COMMANDER TOAD
and the
INTERGALACTIC
SPY

by JANE YOLEN

pictures by BRUCE DEGEN

The Putnam & Grosset Group

For Sandy, our own Tip Toad
  —B.D.

Text copyright © 1986 by Jane Yolen
Illustrations copyright © 1986, 1997 by Bruce Degen
All rights reserved. This book, or parts thereof, may not be reproduced in any form
without permission in writing from the publisher. A PaperStar Book, published in 1997 by
The Putnam & Grosset Group, 200 Madison Avenue, New York, NY 10016.
PaperStar Books and the PaperStar logo are trademarks of
The Putnam Berkley Group, Inc. Originally published in 1986 by
Coward-McCann, Inc. Published simultaneously in Canada.
Printed in the United States of America.

Library of Congress Cataloging-in-Publication Data
Yolen, Jane. Commander Toad and the intergalactic spy.
Summary: Commander Toad and the crew of Star Warts are asked
to rout out Tip Toad, Space Fleet's greatest and most elusive spy.
[1. Toads—Fiction. 2. Science fiction] I. Degen, Bruce, ill.
II. Title. PZ7.Y78 Cmi 1986
ISBN 0-698-11418-3
3 5 7 9 10 8 6 4

For my nephew
John Gregory Yolen
who lives in another world
but sometimes comes here for a visit
—J.Y.

Long green ships
fly through space
past the winking
of a thousand thousand stars.
There is one ship,
one mighty ship,
long and green,
called *Star Warts*.
The captain of this ship
is brave and bright,
bright and brave.
His name is
COMMANDER TOAD.

He guides his ship
where no space ship
has gone before.
To find planets.
To explore galaxies.
To bring a little bit of Earth
out to the alien stars.
But he is not alone
way out in space.

He has a very fine crew.
Mr. Hop
is his copilot.
Lieutenant Lily
runs the ship.
The computer chief
is young Jake Skyjumper.
And old Doc Peeper
in his grass green wig
makes sure everyone
is hoppy and well.

Mr. Hop   Lt. Lily   Jake   Doc Peeper

One day
the commander
calls his crew
all together.
He waves
a piece of paper.
"Star Fleet
is sending us
on a dangerous mission.

Other ships
have gone out
on this mission.
They have not come back."
Lieutenant Lily smiles.
"I am ready,"
she says.

"What is this
dangerous mission?"
asks Mr. Hop.
"We must pick up
a spy.
An intergalactic spy."
Mr. Hop
scratches his head.
Lieutenant Lily asks,
"What is dangerous
about that?"

"This is no
ordinary spy,"
says Commander Toad.
"It is Space Fleet's
greatest spy.
Agent 007½."
"Oooooh,"
says Lieutenant Lily,
"I have heard of him."
"I have, too,"
says Jake.
"His name is Tip Toad.
He is a master of disguise."

"And I know him
even better,"
says Commander Toad.
"He is my cousin.
Even if he is
wearing a disguise,
I will
recognize him,
And so will you.
Everyone in our family
looks alike.
Tip is tall and brown
and toadally handsome."
"Just like you?"
asks Mr. Hop.

Commander Toad
is not amused.
He takes out
a photograph.
In it two small
and brown
and handsome young toads
are on a riverbank
playing hopscotch.

"See for yourself,"
says Commander Toad.
They all look.
"Which one is you,"
asks Lieutenant Lily,
"and which one is Tip Toad?"
The commander just smiles.

"I will plot our course,"
says young Jake.
"Where do we pick up
your famous cousin?"
Commander Toad
shows them all the paper.
It is covered
with strange marks.
"That is Toad Code,"
says Mr. Hop.
"Let me try to read it."
He looks
at the paper
for a very long time.

At last he says,
"Your cousin
is on a planet
called Eden.

Eden is full
of flowers.
And full
of spies.
They are *all*
in disguise."
"All of them?"
asks Doc Peeper.
"It is a spy
convention,"
says Mr. Hop.

"Spies from
all over the galaxy
are dropped off.
They try to trick
one another.
They try to learn
one another's secrets.
Then they try
to escape
and leave the others
behind.

Tip Toad says
no one must see him
without his disguise
or he will be in danger
all the rest
of his life.
He will never be able
to retire
and live on the riverbank
without a disguise."

"Poor Tip,"
says Commander Toad.
There is a tear
in his eye.
"Then we will have
to figure out
which one is Tip,"
says Lieutenant Lily.
"I am ready."

"Here are some clues,"
says Commander Toad.
"Tip will wear
his Star Fleet wristwatch,
the croak-a-dial.
He will drink
Croak-a-Cola.
He will carry
a photograph
of his favorite cousin."

"I will know him,"
says Lily.
"But if we pick up
the wrong spy
and bring that one
on board the ship,
we will all be in danger,"
says Mr. Hop.
"I will know him,"
says Commander Toad.
"And so will you.
Tip and I
look just alike."

Jake finds Eden
on the star map.
Lieutenant Lily
puts the ship
into high wart speed.
Off they go.
The planet Eden
is full of flowers.
Red and orange,
yellow and pink.

Commander Toad
and Lieutenant Lily,
Mr. Hop
and Doc Peeper
climb into
the sky skimmer.
Only Jake Skyjumper
stays behind.

The sky skimmer
floats down,
down, down, down
and lands in a field
of buttercups.
Bees hum.
Birds sing.
It is a lovely world.
They leave the skimmer
and walk around.
They smell the sweet air.

Suddenly,

an enormous monster,

all teeth and tail,

appears before them.

The monster smiles.

His mouth is full

of buttercups

and teeth.

He has 247 big teeth.

He has 73 little teeth.

"Run!" shouts
old Doc Peeper.
He starts to hop
back to the skimmer.
Lieutenant Lily
does not run.
She kneels down
and points her gun
right at the
73 little teeth.

Before she can shoot,
the monster booms out,
"HI, COUSIN HIP!"
"STOP!!!"
shouts Commander Toad.

"Lily, do not shoot.
That monster
is my cousin.
He was Tip-top
and I was Hip-hop.
We looked alike.
We dressed alike.
We spoke alike.
No one
could tell us apart."
"You sure do not
look alike now,"
says Doc Peeper.
"No," admits
Commander Toad.
"Now I am better looking."

"That is a great disguise,"
says Mr. Hop.
Commander Toad
gives his monster cousin
a great big hug.

· 33 ·

Suddenly,
a second monster,
long and slithery,
with 257 big teeth
and 63 little teeth,
slides through the flowers
toward them.
Lieutenant Lily kneels.

She aims her gun.
"Hi, coussssssin Hip,"
hisses the monster.
"STOP!!!" shouts
Commander Toad.
"I have made
a big mistake.
That is my cousin."

"I do not understand,"
says Lieutenant Lily.
"You say your cousin Tip,
master of disguise,
is the only one
who knows your nickname.
But *both* these monsters
know it.
Can they *both* be
Agent 007½?"
"That is a *great* disguise,"
says Mr. Hop.

Suddenly,
three more monsters
with lots of teeth,
both big and little,
stomp through the field
toward the crew.
They shout,
"HI, COUSIN HIP!"
"We have a problem,"
says Lieutenant Lily.

"A monster of a problem,"
adds Doc Peeper.
"I knew this
croak-and-dagger stuff
would not be easy."
"That is a
really
great disguise,"
says Mr. Hop.

All five monsters
are wearing
croak-a-dials.
All five monsters
are sipping
Croak-a-Cola.
All five monsters
are carrying
photographs
of small and brown
and handsome young toads.

"I am your cousin,
Tip Toad,
master of disguise,"
say all five monsters
together.
"These other monsters
are imposters.
They are evil spies
who want to
get on board your ship
and steal it
and all its secrets
away."

They growl
at each other
and smile
toothy smiles
at the *Star Warts* crew.
The crew
climbs quickly
back into the skimmer.
The skimmer lifts off
above the monsters.
Commander Toad needs
time to think,
just out of reach
of monster claws
and monster jaws.

The five monsters
lie back
in the buttercups.
They stick their feet
and tails
in the air,
drink their Croak-a-Cola,
and talk about
the good old days
when they were
hoppy little toads.

"Only one of them
is telling the truth,"
says Mr. Hop wisely.
"That means that
four of them
are lying,"
says Commander Toad,
counting on his fingers.
"But which is which?"

Mr. Hop thinks out loud.
"What does a toad do
that no one else
can do,
even a master
of disguise?"
Commander Toad
leaps up.
The sky skimmer
rocks dangerously
from side to side.
"I have it!"
he shouts.

"Have what?"
asks Mr. Hop.
"The answer
to your question,"
says Commander Toad.
"Quick, Lily,
fly us across Eden
until you find
a field full
of tulips."

Lieutenant Lily
does not ask questions.
She salutes.
"Aye, aye,
Commander Toad,"
she says.

They peer over the side
looking for the field.
"There!"
says Lieutenant Lily
at last.
"I see one."
They look down
and, sure enough,
below them is a field
full of tulips
blowing prettily
in a passing breeze.

Commander Toad
turns and cups
his hands to his mouth.
"Oh, cousin Tip,"
he shouts.
"Come here."
Five monsters
stand up.
Five monsters
come running.
STOMP. STOMP. STOMP.

"I have a test
for all of you,"
says Commander Toad.
"What kind of test?"
The monsters ask.
"I am going to send
Tip Toad
through the tulips,"
says Commander Toad.
Everyone groans.

"What good is that?"
asks Mr. Hop.
"You will see,"
says Commander Toad.
"Monster number one,
start through."

The big monster
with the 247
big teeth
runs through the tulips.
Bees and fleas
buzz around his head.
"Monster number two,"
says Commander Toad,
pointing to the slithery spy.
He slips into the grass
and slides along,
disturbing
wasps and gnats.

"Monsters three and four—
begin,"
calls out Commander Toad.
They humph
and galumph
and stumble
through the tulips.
All around them
little insects
buzz and hum.

"Monster number five,"
calls out
Commander Toad.
The last monster,
fat and striped,
with one dark horn,
lumbers to his feet.
He swaggers
through the field.
He kicks up
seventeen flies.

Then *flick—flick—flick*,
faster than the eye
can follow,
out of his monster mouth
darts a long, sticky tongue.
Flick—flick—flick.
Seventeen times.
Every single fly
disappears.

"He is the one,"
says Commander Toad.
"Only a toad
as smart and as fast
and as handsome
as my cousin Tip
can catch flies
like that."
Old Doc Peeper laughs.
"*He* catches flies
and you catch spies."

"That's some disguise!"
says Mr. Hop.
Lieutenant Lily
pushes a button
and a rope ladder
unfolds.
The bottom rung
is right in front
of Tip Toad's nose.
Quickly he climbs up.

The other monsters
run toward the ladder.
They open their jaws.
They show their claws.
But they are too late.
Agent 007½
climbs aboard the skimmer,
bringing the ladder
up with him.
"Thanks, Cousin Hip "
says the monster.

"I hope I really *am*
your cousin,"
says Commander Toad.
"You will soon know,"
says the monster,
grinning with 412 teeth.
The skimmer lifts up
to the ship.

Once on board,
the monster takes off
his disguise.
He takes off his horn.
He takes off his hair.
He takes off his hide.
He is a tall
and slim
and handsome brown toad.

Commander Toad
puts his arm
around Tip Toad.
"See,"
says the commander.
"We look exactly alike."
Lieutenant Lily smiles.
Mr. Hop shakes his head.
Old Doc Peeper
laughs out loud.
"I do not think
you look *exactly* alike,"
says young Jake.

Commander Toad
looks at his cousin.
He looks at himself
in the mirror.
"You are right,"
says the commander.
"We may look alike,
but I am *much* better looking."

"Give me a minute,"
says Tip Toad,
"and I can be
just as good looking as you.
After all,
I *am*
a master of disguise."

They all laugh.
Then young Jake
sends the green ship
into deep hopper space
and they leapfrog
across the galaxy
from star to star to star.

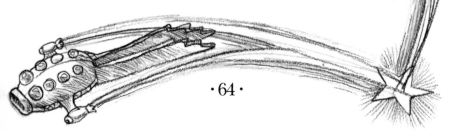